First American Edition 2016
Kane Miller, A Division of EDC Publishing

Text copyright © 2016 Sally Rippin
Illustrations copyright © Alisa Coburn 2016
Logo and design copyright © Hardie Grant Egmont 2016

First published in Australia in 2016 by Hardie Grant Egmont

For information contact:
Kane Miller, A Division of EDC Publishing
P.O. Box 470663
Tulsa, OK 74147-0663

www.kanemiller.com
www.edcpub.com
www.usbornebooksandmore.com

Library of Congress Control Number: 2015960070

Printed and bound in China
1 2 3 4 5 6 7 8 9 10

ISBN: 978-1-61067-554-3

Billie's YUMMY BAKERY ADVENTURE

by Sally Rippin

illustrated by Alisa Coburn

Kane Miller
A DIVISION OF EDC PUBLISHING

Billie B. Brown DRAGS her feet into preschool.

She didn't eat much breakfast, and now she is feeling growly and grumbly.

"Come into the classroom,"
Miss Amy tells Billie. "We're baking!"

Billie runs over to where her friend Emily is arranging cakes on a tray.

Jack comes too.

"Can we join in?" ask Jack and Billie.

Emily frowns.

"There's plenty of
room for all of you,"
says Miss Amy.

She helps Jack
put on an apron.

She gives Billie
a baker's hat to wear.

"And look at all
these hungry toys!"
says Miss Amy.

EMILY'S
BAKERY

Billie and Jack go into the kitchen. They decide to bake button buns.

Billie measures the ingredients, and Jack stirs.

They roll the dough into balls and bake them in the oven.

Soon a **delicious** smell
wafts around the bakery.

Billie carries a tray of hot
buns to the counter.

The customers' noses
sniff and twitch.

Ooh!

Mmmmmm!

Yum!

Everyone wants to taste Billie and Jack's **Scrumptious** button buns.

Emily is jealous. She disappears into the kitchen.

Another **fantabulous** smell fills the air.

Ta-da!

Emily carries out the most spectacular cake you've ever seen!

We can do **better than that,** says Billie.

This time, Billie and Jack make
a batch of pinkle-dough muffins.

Billie adds a *whole* packet of
magic powder to the mix.

She flicks the oven to high.

Then they wait.

QUICK & HOT

Groan Crack

Hiss

BAM!

There are funny sounds coming from the oven.

Billie and Jack take a step back, and then …

Globby, goopy pinkle dough flies everywhere!

What a mess.

The customers storm out the door.

My bakery is RUINED!
cries Emily.

Billie feels terrible.

Just then, Billie has an idea.

A **Super-duper** idea!

She grabs a huge spoon
and the biggest cake pan.

She scrapes …

and scoops …

and pats …

all the pinkle dough into it.

SLOW & STEADY

This time Billie adjusts
the oven carefully.

A **delectable** smell
wafts through the bakery.

Billie and Jack carry the new cake out to Emily.
"I'm sorry I scared off our customers," Billie says.

Emily smiles. "I'm sorry I was so grumpy."

"I was too," says Billie.

"LOOK!" says Jack.
"The customers are
coming back."

Billie, Jack and Emily cut up
the cake and share it all around.

Soon all the cake is gone,
and so are the customers.

So she hangs up the

Closed

sign and wipes
down the counters.

Jack does
the dishes …

and Emily
washes the floors.

Then they open the bakery door …

BAKERY

... and step back
into the classroom.

Just in time for fruit snack.

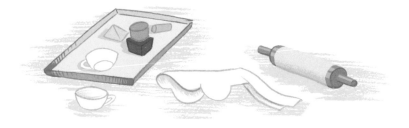